THE
STEADFAST
TIN
SOLDIER

The Steadfast Tin Soldier

By Hans Christian Andersen · Illustrated by Gianni de Conno

PURPLE BEAR BOOKS · NEW YORK

THERE WERE ONCE TWENTY-FIVE TIN SOLDIERS who were all brothers, for they were all made from the same tin spoon. They carried their muskets on their shoulders and looked straight ahead. Their uniforms were red and blue and very pretty indeed. The very first thing they heard in this world, when the lid was taken off their box, was, "Tin soldiers!" for that is what the little boy cried, clapping his hands when he saw them. They had been given to him for his birthday, and he set them up on the table.

All the soldiers were exactly alike except one, who was a little different. He had only one leg, for he was the last to be cast and there had not been enough tin left. But he stood just as steadily on his one leg as the others on their two. And it is just this soldier that this story is all about.

There were a lot of other toys on the table where the soldiers were set up, but the one that really caught the eye was a beautiful castle made of paper. Through the small windows you could see straight into the rooms. Little trees stood outside around a small mirror that represented a lake. Swans made of wax floated on top and were reflected in it. This was very pretty, but prettiest of all was a little maiden who was standing at the open door of the castle. She, too, was made of paper, but she had a skirt of the finest gauze and a little narrow blue ribbon over her shoulders like a scarf, with a glittering spangle in the middle that was as large as her face. The little maiden stretched out her arms, for she was a dancer, and she lifted one of her legs so high that the tin soldier could not see it at all and thought that she had only one leg, like himself.

She is the wife for me! he thought. But she is so grand and lives in a castle. I have only a box and that belongs to all twenty-five of us. That is no place for her. But I would like to make her acquaintance all the same. So he lay down at full length behind a snuff-box where he could easily watch the charming little maiden, who kept standing on one leg without losing her balance.

Toward evening, all the other tin soldiers were put into their box and the people in the house went to bed. Then the toys began to play, paid visits, went to war, and gave balls. The tin soldiers rattled in their box, for they wanted to join in the fun, but they could not get the lid off.

The nutcrackers turned somersaults, the slate pencil was at work on the slate. There was so much noise that the canary woke up and joined in the chatter, but he spoke in verse. The only two who did not move from their places were the tin soldier and the little dancer. She stood straight up on the tip of her toe, with both arms stretched out, and the tin soldier stood just as firmly on his one leg and did not take his eyes off her even for a moment.

The clock struck twelve, then *bang*! off went the lid of the snuff-box. There was no snuff in it, only a tiny black goblin, for it was really a kind of jack-in-the-box. "Tin soldier," said the goblin, "please keep your eyes to yourself!" But the tin soldier pretended not to hear. "Well, just you wait until tomorrow!" said the goblin.

When the children came down in the morning, the tin soldier was put on the windowsill, and whether it was the goblin or the draft that did it, all of a sudden the window flew up and the soldier fell head over heels from the third story.

He fell at a terrible rate and landed on his helmet, with his only leg straight up in the air and his bayonet stuck between the paving stones. The housemaid and the little boy went down immediately to look for him, but they couldn't see him anywhere, although they nearly stepped on him.

If only the little tin soldier had cried, "Here I am," they might have found him, but he did not think it proper to call out when he was in uniform.

Then it began to rain. The drops fell harder and harder until it became a real downpour. When it was over, two boys came along. "Just look," said one, "here's a tin soldier. Let us send him for a sail." So they made a little boat out of newspaper, put the tin soldier in the middle, and there he was, sailing down the gutter. Both the boys ran alongside and clapped their hands.

Goodness me, what large waves there were in that gutter and how strong the current was! But then it *had* been a real downpour.

The paper boat was tossed up and down, and now and then it turned round and round, until the tin soldier was quite dizzy, but he was steadfast and didn't move a muscle. He just looked straight ahead and shouldered his musket. All at once the boat drifted into a storm drain and plunged into a sewer that was just as dark as it had been inside the tin soldier's box. Where am I going now? he wondered. Oh, this must be the goblin's fault! If only the little maiden were here in the boat, I would not mind if it were twice as dark.

Suddenly he came upon a big water rat, who lived in the sewer. "Where is your passport?" demanded the rat. "Let me have it!" The tin soldier said not a word and held his musket tighter than ever. Away went the boat, and the rat after it. Ugh! How he gnashed his teeth and called out to the leaves and twigs, "Stop him, stop him! He hasn't paid the toll and hasn't shown his passport!"

But the current grew stronger and stronger, and the tin soldier could now see daylight shining at the end of the sewer. He heard a roaring sound that would have frightened even the boldest of men, for just where the sewer ended, the water poured out into a large canal, and this was just as dangerous for him as it would be for us to be carried over a great waterfall.

He was now so near it that he could not stop, so the boat swept out into the canal. The poor tin soldier stiffened himself as well as he could, and no one could say that he even moved an eyelid. The boat whirled round three or four times, filled with water, and began to sink. The tin soldier stood up to his neck in water, and the boat sank deeper and deeper. The paper grew more and more sodden, until the water went over the soldier's head. He thought of the charming little dancer, whom he would never see again, and an old song rang in his ears:

> *Oh, warrior bold, good-bye!*
> *Thy end, alas, is nigh.*

Then the paper boat fell apart and the tin soldier tumbled right through and was instantly gobbled up by a big fish. Oh, how dark it was in there, even worse than in the storm drain, and there was so little room! But the tin soldier was steadfast and lay at full length with his musket on his shoulder. The fish darted about in the most alarming way. Then it lay quite still.

Suddenly there was a flash like lightning. Daylight appeared, and someone cried, "Tin soldier!" The fish had been caught, taken to the market, sold, and brought to a kitchen, where the cook cut it up with a big knife. She took the soldier and marched him into the sitting room where everyone wanted to see this remarkable man who had been traveling about inside a fish. The tin soldier wasn't at all proud. He thought nothing of it.

They stood him up on the table, and oh, what curious things do happen in the world! The tin soldier was in the very same room where he had been before! He saw the same children, and the same toys were standing on the table—the pretty castle and the lovely little dancer who was still poised on one leg while the other was high up in the air. She was steadfast, too. This so touched the tin solder that he was almost ready to weep tin tears, but of course that would not have been at all proper. He looked at her and she looked at him, but they said nothing.

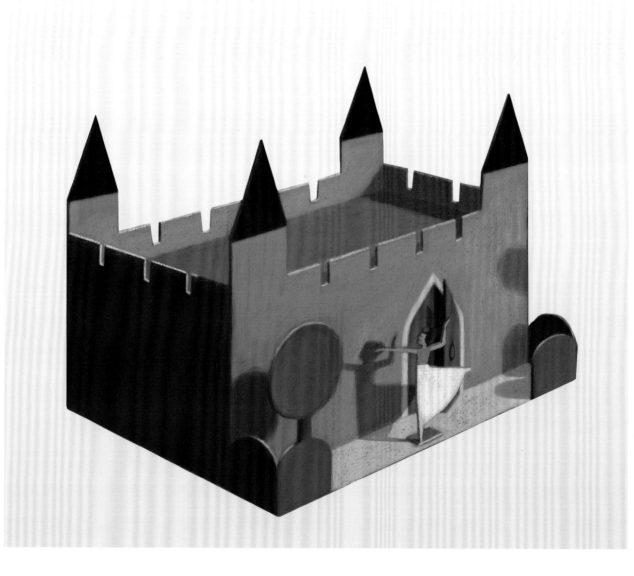

Then one of the little boys took the soldier and threw him into the fireplace. He did not give any reason for doing this. It must have been the fault of the goblin in the snuffbox. The tin soldier was engulfed in flames and felt tremendous heat, but if it came from the actual fire or from his burning love for the little dancer, he did not know. His bright colors were gone, and whether this had happened from his travels or from sorrow no one could tell. He looked at the little maiden and she looked at him. He felt that he was melting, but he still stood there, as steadfast as ever, and shouldered his musket. Suddenly the door flew open, the draft took hold of the dancer, and she flew like a sylph straight into the fireplace, landing right next to the tin soldier. She burst into flames and was gone.

The tin soldier melted into a lump, and when the housemaid swept out the ashes the next day she found him, transformed into a little tin heart.

Of the dancer nothing was left but the little spangle, which was burnt as black as a cinder.

Adapted from the translation by W. Angeldorff

Text copyright © 2006 by Purple Bear Books Inc.

Illustrations copyright © 2006 by Gianni de Conno

First published in Taiwan in 2006 by Grimm Press

First English-language edition published in 2006 by Purple Bear Books Inc., New York.

For more information about our books, visit our website: purplebearbooks.com

Library of Congress Cataloging-in-Publication Data is available.

This edition prepared by Cheshire Studio.

Trade edition

ISBN-10: 1-933327-24-3

ISBN-13: 978-1-933327-24-2

1 3 5 7 9 TE 10 8 6 4 2

Library edition

ISBN-10: 1-933327-25-1

ISBN-13: 978-1-933327-25-9

1 3 5 7 9 LE 10 8 6 4 2

Printed in Taiwan